THE UGLY DUCKLING

HANS CHRISTIAN ANDERSEN
THE UGLY DUCKLING

RETOLD BY
STEPHEN MITCHELL

PAINTINGS BY
STEVE JOHNSON AND LOU FANCHER

CANDLEWICK PRESS
CAMBRIDGE, MASSACHUSETTS

To Brianna Elizabeth Lear and Madeline Rose Lear
S. M.

For Melinda and her family
S. J. & L. F.

It was a glorious day in the countryside. Summer had come, the corn stood golden in the fields, the oats were tall and green, the hay had been stacked in the meadows, and the stork walked on his long red legs, chattering in Egyptian (which was the language he'd learned from his mother). Around the fields and meadows were vast forests, and in the middle of the forests were deep lakes. Yes, it really was a glorious day.

There, in the sunshine, stood an old farmhouse with a moat around it, and from its wall down to the water, large burdock plants grew. The largest were so tall that little children could stand upright underneath them. It was a spot as wild as the thickest forest. Here, a duck sat on her nest, waiting for her ducklings to hatch.

But they were taking such a long time and she had been
sitting for so many days that she was starting to get impatient.
How much longer would this go on? And didn't the other ducks
realize that she would like a little company now and then? But no—
they went right on swimming in the moat and having a wonderful
time, and they were never considerate enough to come by and
sit down with her for a nice chat under the burdock leaves.

Finally, one egg cracked, then
another, then another, until six of them
had cracked open. "Peep, peep!" they
said. The yolks had suddenly come to life,
and each one stuck its little head out of the shell.

"Quack, quack!" said the mother duck encouragingly, and the
ducklings all crawled out as well as they could and looked around at the
green leaves. The mother duck let them look as much as they wanted
to, because green is good for the eyes.

"How big the world is!" said all the ducklings.
And certainly they had a lot more room now
than when they were inside the eggs.

"Do you suppose this is the whole
world?" said the mother duck. "The world
is much bigger than you can imagine: it goes
far past the other side of the garden, right
into the parson's field. But I've never gone as far
as that." She paused. "Are you all out yet?" she said,
standing up. "Ah, not all of you.
The largest egg still hasn't
cracked open. How much
more time is it going to
take? I'm so tired of
sitting here." And she
sat back down on her nest.

"Hello, my dear. How are you doing?" said an old duck who had come to pay the mother duck a visit.

"One of my eggs is taking a very long time to hatch," said the mother duck. "It still doesn't have a single crack in it. But just look at the others. Aren't they the prettiest little ducklings you've ever seen? They all look like their father, that rascal, who never comes to visit me."

"Let me take a look at that egg, the one that won't crack," said the old duck. "Well, of course—it's a turkey egg! Trust me. I was once tricked that way, and I had so much trouble with the little ones. Imagine—they were all afraid of the water. I just couldn't get them to go in. I pleaded, I begged, I snapped and I slapped, but nothing worked. Let me look again. Yes, it's definitely a turkey egg. Take my advice—just leave it to fend for itself, and go teach your real children how to swim."

"Oh, I think I'll sit on it a little longer," the mother duck said. "I've been sitting here so long that a few more days won't matter."

"Suit yourself," said the old duck, and she walked away.

At last the large egg cracked open. "Peep, peep!" said the duckling, and crawled out. He was very big and very ugly. The mother duck stared at him. "What an awfully big duckling!" she said. "None of the others look like this. Could he be a turkey chick after all? Well, we'll find out soon enough. He'll go into the water, even if I have to push him in myself."

The next day was gorgeous, with a bright sun shining down onto the burdock leaves. The mother duck walked down to the water with her whole family and dived in with a splash. "Quack, quack!" she said, and one after another the ducklings jumped in after her. The water closed over their heads, but they came up again in an instant and swam around beautifully, their little legs paddling under them in the most natural way in the world. They were all in the water, and the ugly gray duckling was in the water too, swimming along with the others.

"No, he's definitely not a turkey chick," said the mother duck. "Look how easily he paddles and how straight he holds himself in the water! No doubt about it: he's my own child. And he's quite handsome when you really look at him. Quack, quack! Now children, come along with me and I will take you into society and introduce you to the most important ducks. But you must stay close to me or someone will step on you. And be especially careful around the cat!"

When they reached the duck yard, there was a terrible uproar: two families were fighting over an eel's head. Finally, it was the cat who got it.

"See? That's the way of the world," said the mother duck, licking her beak, for she would have liked to have the eel's head herself.

"Come now, hurry up," she said, "and make a nice bow to that old duck over there. She is the most distinguished duck in the yard. Can you see how proud and aristocratic she is? She's the center of attention wherever she goes. Hurry up, now. And don't turn your feet inward that way. A well-brought-up duckling turns his feet *out,* just like his father and mother. Look: just like this. Now make a nice bow and say, 'Quack!'"

The ducklings did as they were told. But the other ducks glared at them and said, "Will you look at that! One more family trying to invade the yard—as if there weren't enough of us already. And look at that deformed duckling. What a horror! We won't put up with creatures like that." And one duck flew at him and bit him in the neck.

"Leave him alone!" said the mother. "He's not bothering anyone."

"True," said the duck who had bitten him, "but he's too big and ugly. We just don't want him around."

"Pretty children you have, my dear," said the old aristocratic duck. "All but that one. He's rather a dud, don't you think? I wish you could remake him."

"That's not possible, madam," said the mother duck. "He may not be pretty, but he has a very good heart. He's kind and considerate, and that's worth at least as much as good looks. And he can swim as well as the others, perhaps even better. And I have a feeling that he'll be better-looking as he grows up; maybe he'll even get to be a bit smaller. It's just that he stayed too long in his egg. That's why he's not quite the right shape." And she stroked his neck and smoothed his feathers. "Anyway," she said, "I'm sure he'll grow up strong and be able to manage quite well."

"The other ducklings are lovely, though," said the old duck. "Now, make yourselves at home, my dear, and if you happen to find an eel's head, you may bring it to me." And so they made themselves at home.

But the duckling who had come out of his egg last, and who looked so ugly, was bitten and pushed and laughed at by all the other ducks, and by the chickens as well. "What a monster he is!" they all said. And the turkey (who, because he had been born with spurs on his feet, thought he was the emperor of the barnyard) puffed himself up like a ship with full sails and rushed straight at the duckling, gobbling, his face red with anger. The duckling didn't know where to hide. He was very sad to be so ugly that everyone in the barnyard despised him.

That's how the first day was, and afterward it went from bad to worse. The duckling was attacked by everyone. Even his brothers and sisters were mean to him and said, "We hope the cat catches you, you ugly thing!" And his mother, no longer able to bear it, said, "I wish you were far, far away." And the ducks bit him, and the chickens pecked him, and the girl who fed the animals pushed him away with her foot.

So he ran away and flew over the hedge, and the little birds fluttered up out of the bushes, frightened. *They're scared of me because I'm so ugly,* thought the duckling, and he closed his eyes, but he kept on flying. Eventually he came to the great marsh where the wild ducks lived, and he spent the night there, tired and miserable.

In the morning, the wild ducks flew up and looked at their new companion. "What kind of bird are you?" they asked, and the duckling turned around to them all and greeted them as well as he could.

"You're remarkably ugly!" said the wild ducks. "But that doesn't matter to us, as long as you don't marry into our family." The little duckling was hardly thinking of getting married. All he wanted was permission to lie among the reeds and drink a little marsh water.

After he had been there for a couple of days, two wild geese arrived, or rather, two wild ganders (they were both males). They hadn't been hatched for very long; that's why they were so brash.

"Listen, chum," one of them said, "you're so ugly that I like you. Why don't you fly along with us?"

Suddenly there was a *bang, bang!* above them, and the two wild ganders fell down dead among the reeds. *Bang, bang!* sounded again, and flocks of wild geese flew up out of the reeds, and the shots burst out again. It was the first hunt of the season. The hunters surrounded the marsh; some even sat in the branches of the trees that stretched out over the water. The blue smoke from their guns drifted like clouds into the trees and far out over the water, and the hunting dogs splashed into the marsh, bending the reeds on all sides.

The duckling was terrified. He turned his head to hide it beneath his wing, but at that very moment a huge dog passed near him, its long tongue hanging from its mouth and its huge eyes glittering horribly. It thrust its snout very close to the duckling, bared its sharp teeth, and . . . *splash!* away it went without touching him.

"Thank goodness!" sighed the duckling. "I am so ugly that even the dogs won't bite me." And he lay quite still while gun after gun fired and the shots whizzed through the reeds.

It was late in the day before everything was quiet again, but the duckling still didn't dare to get up; he waited several more hours before he looked around, and then he hurried out of the marsh as fast as he could. He ran across meadow and field, but a storm arose and the wind blew so hard that he had trouble getting anywhere.

Toward evening he reached a poor little cottage, which was so broken-down that it couldn't decide which way to fall, and so it remained standing. The storm howled around the duckling so furiously that the only way not to be blown over was to sit down. But then he noticed that the door had come off one of its hinges and was hanging so crookedly that he could crawl into the cottage through the crack. And that's just what he did.

In the cottage lived an old woman with her cat and her hen. The cat, whose name was Sonny, would arch his back and purr; he could even give out sparks, but for that you had to pet his fur the wrong way, from tail to head. The hen had very short little legs, so she was called Chickie Shortlegs. She laid good eggs, and the old woman loved her as if she were her own daughter.

In the morning, they noticed the strange duckling, and the cat began to purr and the hen began to cluck.

"What is it?" said the woman, looking around. But her eyesight wasn't very good, and she thought the duckling was a wild duck who had lost its way. "What a find!" she said. "Now I can have duck eggs, if only it's not a male. We'll have to wait and see." And so the duckling was taken, on trial, for three weeks. But no eggs appeared.

Now, the cat was master of the house and the hen was mistress, and they always said, "Us and the world," because they believed they were half the world, and the better half too. The duckling thought there might be a different opinion about that, but the hen wouldn't hear of it. "Can you lay eggs?" she said.

"No."

"Then be quiet, please."

And the cat said, "Can you arch your back and purr and give out sparks?"

"No."

"Then you have no right to an opinion when sensible people are talking."

So the duckling sat in the corner, in very low spirits. Then he remembered the fresh air and the sunshine, and he felt such a strange longing to swim in the water that he couldn't help telling the hen.

"What's the matter with you?" she said. "You don't have anything to do—that's why you're getting such a silly idea. Lay eggs or purr, and it will pass."

"But it's so wonderful to swim in the water!" said the duckling. "And so glorious to feel it close over your head as you dive down to the bottom!"

"Some pleasure *that* would be!" said the hen. "You must be crazy! Ask the cat—he's the smartest animal I know. Ask him if *he'd* like to swim in the water or dive to the bottom. I won't tell you my own opinion. But ask our mistress, the old woman—there's no one in the world smarter than she is. Do you think *she* would like to swim and let the water close over her head?"

"You don't understand me," said the duckling.

"Well, if *we* don't understand you, who could? You don't think, do you, that you're smarter than the cat or the old woman, not to mention myself? Don't be silly, child. You should thank your good fortune for coming to this place. Don't you have a warm house now, and companions you can learn from? But you're a ninny, and it's not much fun being around you. Believe me, I'm speaking only for your own good. I'm telling you unpleasant truths, and that's how we can recognize our real friends. Take my advice: just learn how to lay eggs, or purr and give out sparks."

"I think I'll go out into the wide world," said the duckling.

"Go ahead," said the hen.

So the duckling went. He swam in the water and dived. But all the other animals avoided him because he was so ugly.

Then autumn came. The leaves in the forest turned yellow and brown; the wind took them and danced them around in the air in every direction. High up, it became very cold; the clouds hung down heavy with snowflakes and hail, and on the fence the raven stood and cried "Ow! Ow!" because he was so cold. The little duckling was having a very hard time.

One evening, as the sun set, a flock of large, magnificent birds appeared out of the bushes. The duckling had never seen anything so beautiful; they were dazzlingly white, with long graceful necks. They uttered an extraordinary cry, spread their gorgeous long wings, and flew away from that cold place to warmer lands, to open lakes. They flew up so high, so high, and the ugly little duckling felt a strange feeling as he watched them. He turned around and around in the water like a wheel, stretched his neck high in the air toward them, and uttered a cry so loud and so strange that he himself was frightened by it.

Oh, he would never forget those beautiful, happy birds, and as soon as they were out of his sight, he dived to the bottom of the water, and when he came up again, he was beside himself with joy. He had no idea what kind of birds they were, or where they had flown to, but he loved them more than anyone he had ever known. And he didn't envy them at all—how could he ever dream of such loveliness for himself? He would have been content if only the ducks had allowed him to stay with them, as ugly as he was.

The winter was so cold, so cold. The duckling had to keep swimming around in the water so that it wouldn't freeze completely, but every night the hole he swam in got smaller and smaller. The weather was so cold that the ice in the water crackled as he swam, and the duckling had to paddle continuously to keep the hole from closing. At last he was too exhausted to paddle. He lay still and froze into the ice.

Early the next morning, a peasant arrived. When he saw the duckling, he broke the ice with his wooden shoe and took the duckling home to his wife. There the duckling warmed up and came back to life.

The peasant's children wanted to play with him, but the duckling thought they were trying to hurt him. Frightened, he jumped and ran straight into the milk bowl, and the milk spilled all over the floor. The woman shrieked and clapped her hands, and then he flew into the butter tub and then down into the flour bin and out again. How funny he looked when he came out! The woman screamed and swung at him with the fire tongs; the children ran and tripped over each other trying to catch him, laughing and shouting. Luckily, the door was open, and the duckling slipped out and hid among the bushes in the newly fallen snow and lay there, exhausted.

It would be too sad to describe all the misery that the duckling
had to endure during that harsh winter. When the sun finally began
to get warm again, he was lying among the reeds in the marsh.
The larks sang. It was glorious spring.

Suddenly the duckling spread his wings, which beat more strongly than before and carried him swiftly away. Before he knew it, he found himself in a large garden, where the apple trees were in bloom and the fragrant lilacs bent their long green branches down to the winding streams. It was so beautiful here in all the freshness of spring!

And straight ahead, out of the thicket, came three splendid white birds, like the ones he had seen last autumn. They rustled their feathers and swam so lightly on the water. The duckling recognized them and was overcome with a strange excitement.

"I will fly to those royal birds! It doesn't matter if they bite me or drive me away; I just want to be with them for a moment. They are so beautiful."

And he flew out onto the water and swam toward the magnificent creatures. When they saw him, they rushed to him with outstretched wings.

"It's all right," said the duckling. "You can bite me if you want. I don't mind," and he bent his head down to the water and waited for them.

But what did he see in the clear water? It had to be his own reflection—there was no question about that. But why wasn't he seeing a clumsy, ugly, dark-gray bird reflected in the water? It was impossible, it was too good to be true, but what was reflected in the water was the image of one of those glorious birds! Could it be? He looked again, and the image was still in front of him, looking back at him from the water. It must be him. How incredible! How wonderful! How grateful he felt!

He was just like those gorgeous creatures swimming toward him. He was one of them. At last he belonged. He gave thanks for all the misery he had undergone, which made him all the more grateful for his happiness now. And the three birds swam around him and stroked him with their beaks.

Some little children came into the garden and threw bread and grain into the water, and the littlest shouted, "There's a new one!" And the other children, delighted, said, "Yes, a new swan has come!" And they clapped their hands and danced around and ran to get their father and mother, and they all threw bread and cake into the water and said, "The new one is the most beautiful swan of all— so young and so magnificent!"

This made him feel so shy that he hid his head beneath his wing. He didn't know what to do—he was so happy. But he was not at all conceited, for a good heart never becomes conceited. He remembered how persecuted and ridiculed he had been, and now he heard everyone say that he was the most beautiful of all the beautiful swans. Even the lilacs bent their branches to him, right down to the water, and the sun shone so warm and so bright. Then he rustled his feathers, raised his slender neck, and, with a full heart, he rejoiced: "I never dreamed of such happiness as this when I was the ugly duckling!"